For Cheryl, the Brave
–S.C.

To Dad, with love
–E.U.

An imprint of Rodale Books
733 Third Avenue, New York, NY 10017
Visit us online at RodaleKids.com.

Text © 2018 by Suzy Capozzi
Illustrations © 2018 by Eren Unten

Rodale Kids books may be purchased for business or promotional use
or for special sales. For information, please e-mail: RodaleKids@Rodale.com.

Printed in China
Manufactured by RRD Asia 201801

Design by Amy C. King
Text set in Report School
The artwork for this book was created with pencil and paper,
then painted digitally in Adobe Photoshop.

Library of Congress Cataloging-in-Publication Data is on file with the publisher.

ISBN 978–1–62336–954–5 paperback
ISBN 978–1–62336–956–9 hardcover

Distributed to the trade by Macmillan
10 9 8 7 6 5 4 3 2 1 paperback
10 9 8 7 6 5 4 3 2 1 hardcover

I am Brave

RODALE KiDS

We are going on a trip.
It is my first time on a plane.
I am a little nervous.
So I try to read a book.

Tim calls me **Scaredy Kat**.
Mom tells Tim to buckle up
and behave.

I close my eyes.
The plane takes off.

It feels like a roller coaster.
I like roller coasters.
I'm not scared anymore. I am brave.

We unpack at the hotel.

Then we go to the pool.
Tim and I head for the waterslide.

At the top, we get in a tube.
It looks like a **wild** river below.
But Tim leads the way, and I let go.

8

We splash and laugh the whole way down.
We are brave.

The next day, we go horseback riding.
My horse's name is Big Ben.
How will I get up there?
Will I fall off his back?

A teacher shows me the ropes.
I trust Big Ben and he trusts me.

Later, we ride on the beach.
Big Ben and I make a good team.
I am brave.

Another day, we hike
in the woods.
We see birds and lizards.

We climb down to a spooky cave.
Mom won't go in.
Maybe I will stay with her.

I decide to go inside.
It is dark and cool.
There are tiny holes in the
top of the cave.

They look like stars.
We see some bats, too.
They don't scare me.
I am brave.

It is the last day of our trip.
Mom says the waves are
perfect for surfing.

First, we practice on the beach.

In the water, Mom shows us how
to stand up.

Dad shows us how to belly flop.

We paddle out.
A big wave comes in.
I take a deep breath
and exhale slowly.

I can do this.
I jump up on my board.

I catch the wave!
I am brave.

That night, we go to a party.
The food looks strange.

I try it. It's yummy!
After we eat, everyone dances.

There is a magic show, too.
The magician needs help.
We all raise our hands.

He picks me!

I put on a cape and get into the big box.
It is very dark inside, but I'm not afraid.

The magician waves his wand.

He opens the box. It is empty.
Everyone gasps.

Ta-da!
I'm back!

Tim wants to know the magician's secret.
I'll never tell.
He gives me a **new** nickname—
Kat the Brave.
Tim is right.
I am brave!

When do YOU feel brave?

Can you think of three examples?

Also available:

I Am Strong

Look for these other titles in the
POSITIVE POWER series:
- **I Am Thankful**
- **I Am Kind**
- **I Am Smart**
- **I Am Helpful**

To learn more about Rodale Kids Curious Readers,
please visit RodaleKids.com.